A Note to Parents and Caregivers:

Read-it! Readers are for children who are just starting on the amazing road to reading. These beautiful books support both the acquisition of reading skills and the love of books.

The PURPLE LEVEL presents basic topics and objects using high frequency words and simple language patterns.

The RED LEVEL presents familiar topics using common words and repeating sentence patterns.

The BLUE LEVEL presents new ideas using a larger vocabulary and varied sentence structure.

The YELLOW LEVEL presents more challenging ideas, a broad vocabulary, and wide variety in sentence structure.

The GREEN LEVEL presents more complex ideas, an extended vocabulary range, and expanded language structures.

The ORANGE LEVEL presents a wide range of ideas and concepts using challenging vocabulary and complex language structures.

When sharing a book with your child, read in short stretches, pausing often to talk about the pictures. Have your child turn the pages and point to the pictures and familiar words. And be sure to reread favorite stories or parts of stories.

There is no right or wrong way to share books with children. Find time to read with your child, and pass on the legacy of literacy.

Adria F. Klein, Ph.D.
Professor Emeritus
California State University
San Bernardino, California

Editor: Jill Kalz
Designer: Tracy Kaehler
Page Production: Melissa Kes
Creative Director: Keith Griffin
Editorial Director: Carol Jones
The illustrations in this book were created digitally.

Picture Window Books
5115 Excelsior Boulevard
Suite 232
Minneapolis, MN 55416
877-845-8392
www.picturewindowbooks.com

Printed in the United States of America.

Library of Congress Cataloging-in-Publication Data
Shaskan, Trisha Speed.
The ticket / by Trisha Speed Shaskan ; illustrated by James Demski Jr.
p. cm. — (Read-it! readers)
Summary: One morning, Sally finds a ticket next to her bed but does not know what
it is for until she takes a walk with her parents, looking for clues.
ISBN-13: 978-1-4048-2423-2 (hardcover)
ISBN-10: 1-4048-2423-5 (hardcover)
[1. Surprise—Fiction. 2. Circus—Fiction. 3. Mystery and detective stories.]
I. Demski, James, 1976– ill. II. Title. III. Series.
PZ7.S53242Tic 2006
[E]—dc22
                                                          2006003385

The Ticket

by Trisha Speed Shaskan
illustrated by James Demski Jr.

Special thanks to our advisers for their expertise:

Adria F. Klein, Ph.D.
Professor Emeritus, California State University
San Bernardino, California

Susan Kesselring, M.A.
Literacy Educator
Rosemount–Apple Valley–Eagan (Minnesota) School District

PICTURE WINDOW BOOKS
Minneapolis, Minnesota

One morning, Sally found a red-and-white striped ticket next to her bed. She quickly got dressed and ran to the kitchen.

Sally showed the ticket to her parents.

"What is this for?" Sally asked.

"It's for something very exciting," her mom said.

"Let's go look for clues," her dad said.

Sally and her parents walked down the block.
They saw a giant picture of an elephant.

"Look at the elephant!" Sally said.

"It looks big and strong," her mom said.

"It looks friendly, too," her dad said.

Sally looked down at the ground and saw crushed peanut shells.

"Look at the shells!" Sally said.

"It looks like someone has been eating peanuts," her mom said.

"Someone must have been hungry," her dad said.

Sally looked across the street and saw lots of colorful balloons.

"Look at the balloons!" Sally said.

"They're pretty," her mom said.

"I wonder what those are for," her dad said.

"Look at the clown!" Sally said.

"I think he's too big for that small car. He looks silly," her mom said.

"I wonder where he's going," her dad said.

15

Sally and her parents came to a red-and-white striped tent. Sally heard music and a loud voice.

17

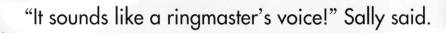

"It sounds like a ringmaster's voice!" Sally said.

"What does a ringmaster do?" her mom and dad asked.

18

19

Sally smiled. She pulled the red-and-white striped ticket out of her pocket.

Her parents pulled tickets out of their pockets, too.

"A ringmaster welcomes people to the circus!"
Sally said.

"Surprise, Sally!" her parents said.

23

More *Read-it!* Readers

Bright pictures and fun stories help you practice your reading skills. Look for more books at your level.

Looking for a specific title or level? A complete list of *Read-it!* Readers is available on our Web site:

www.picturewindowbooks.com